T0146917

Satan's Return and the Trial of God

(on Earth)

God must be punished.

JEMADARI VI-BEE-KIL KILELE

Other Books by Jemadari Vi-Bee-Kil Kilele

- ❖ **The Serial Killer**
- ❖ **The Private Secretary**
- ❖ **The Trial of Satan**
- ❖ **The Pong of the Father**
- ❖ **Ascension of Satan**
- ❖ **Spleen & Lullabies**
- ❖ **La Bile Echauffée (available in French version.)**

Satan's Return and the Trial of God *(on Earth) adds a new page to the controversial trilogy of Satan, grappling with allegations leveled against him by God and manipulated human beings.*

Order this book online at www.trafford.com
or email orders@trafford.com

Most Trafford titles are also available at major online book retailers.

Printed in the United States of America.

ISBN: 978-1-4907-0555-2 (sc)
ISBN: 978-1-4907-0557-6 (hc)
ISBN: 978-1-4907-0556-9 (e)

Library of Congress Control Number: 2013911338

Trafford rev. 07/17/2013

 www.trafford.com

North America & international
toll-free: 1 888 232 4444 (USA & Canada)
fax: 812 355 4082

CONTENTS

LIST OF CHARACTERS

1. The Crowd (out of the court room and in the passageway)
2. Security Officer
3. Court Porter
4. First man
5. Second man
6. First Woman
7. Lawyer
8. Second Woman
9. Public Prosecutor
10. Satan
11. Court Orderly
12. Judge President
13. Two assessors
14. Priest(God Incarnate)
15. Other Clerical members
16. The Public gallery
17. René Descartes

18. Joseph Stalin
19. Karl Marx
20. Voltaire
21. Jean-Paul Sartre.

God must be punished.

FOREWORD

Return of Satan . . . is the last (third) book in this trilogy dealing with the conflict between God and Satan. It comes to close the whole series and ends with an unexpected verdict against the almighty God that we all blindly revere. Here, God is being tried for his failure to keep his promises tendered to the humanity, therefore bailing out Mr. Satan;___ whom for too long has been a victim of an organized blackmailing campaign by God and his "Ministers" scattered all over the world.

The Trial of Satan, Ascension of Satan and *Satan's Return and the Trial of God (on Earth)* in a whole series is a fiction. It is a compact, powerful, provocative and frightening piece of literature which has never been written before in our lifetime. George Orwell would say *"Freedom is the right to tell people what they hate to hear."* And, it is that freedom that has motivated the author to philosophically tackle a subject which is taboo and unimaginable to many whose faith is put to test here.

For more than 2000 years, since Christianity exists, enough books have been written, almost all in praise of the Lord____ God. Plenty books to fill a library. And to my knowledge, not one has dared defend the cause of the Devil, otherwise known as Satan, Lucifer, Demon, etc.

While the author's aim is not totally to shift the minds of religions' staunch believers; this trilogy, to my feelings, attempts to question the one official side of the story that we have been used to: *"Satan is bad and God is good."* However, the goodness of God has never thwarted the "badness" of Satan! So, if Satan and God were old buddies? One wonders then why naïve and "fanaticised" human beings should be perpetually losing their lives in a bottomless quarrel ignited by two old chaps.

With poignant biblical references to support Satan's arguments in court room, the reader soon learns that Mr. God owes much to his alleged beloved yet suffering human beings.

Jemadari Vi-Bee-Kil Kilele

SATAN'S RETURN AND THE TRIAL OF GOD (*ON EARTH*)

God must be punished.

ACT 1: SCENE 1

[A crowd is gathered outside the Magistrate court house, chatting. Some people are entering while others are coming out. The gate security officer is checking those who are entering; instructing them to drop their hand bags and all other items on the tray one by one.]

Porter:

Next *[A great number of persons enter the court house and start reading the lists of court appearances displayed on the wall notice board.]*

First man:

This is unusual! Just read this. *[To those who surround him.]*

Second man:

What's up?

First man:

We were not informed about all this. This announcement [*Removing forcibly the paper from the notice board*] says "*all court appearances today have been cancelled.*" Look at this, buddy!

First man:

But why?

First woman:

But why? It's so strange!

Second man:

Why not sending us SMS messages prior to this anarchy? We have each of us a lot of things to do out there, instead; they have wasted our time by letting us come up to here and attend an appearance of a case which does not concern us.

First woman:

What do you think? It's a sign of incompetence.

First man:

It's just disgusting; you know? Only one case is on the role today.

[Heading towards the court room, a lawyer comes behind and reacts to the first man's utterances]: Yeah, take it as it is.

First man:

What do you mean?

Lawyer:

The whole court has decided like that.

Second woman:

What?

Lawyer:

Owing to the magnitude of this case which you deem "*does not concern you*"; all other cases have been cancelled; adjourned for ulterior date, yet to be announced. You should know that this is an exceptional case in the history of our justice system. Just read that grand title over there *[Pointing at the notice board]* and you'll tell me what is what.

Crowd: *[Approaching the notice board]*

"Trial of God."

One man in the crowd:

And, who's the plaintiff if I may so ask?

Crowd:

Yes, yes, say it again. Who is the complainant, sir?

Lawyer:

The plaintiff?

Crowd:

Yeah.

Lawyer:

[Leaving the crowd] It's the devil. Mr. Satan. He's here; and some human beings too are backing him. They all have a case against God. You should attend; ladies and gentlemen. I mean, all of us should . . .

Crowd:

Mr. Satan? What a curse? [*Many start screaming and running away from the place. The lawyer proceeds in the alley and leaves the place]*. Satan, Satan, Devil, Lucifer; oh, that evil man.

Lawyer:

Follow me if you want. Only one courtroom number, the biggest one is open today. Come through.

[In a frenzied commotion, many entrants rush to court room no 1.]

Crowd: *[Some individuals murmuring.]*

This could be a sensational trial ladies and gentlemen. Let us go and attend.

Second man:

It's gonna be fireworks between God and Satan.

Crowd:

God versus Satan, God versus Satan . . . what a trial this is gonna be!

ACT 1: SCENE 2

[The courtroom is fully packed to rafters. Some people get seated while others are standing up.]

Public Prosecutor: *[Calling names from a file list]*

Mr. Satan.

Satan:

Here I am.

Public Prosecutor.

God*[Everyone in the hall looks left and right, then all turn suspicious of one another]*

Mr or rather Ms, oh! Sorry Mrs. God *[The audience laughs]*. Are you here? Oh! It seems there is no Mr. God in the court room?

(*Enter the court Judge President and two assessors*)

Court Orderly:

All rise (*The court rise in honour of the court Judge President*)

Court Orderly:

Thank you. Please, get seated.

Judge President:

Mr. Public prosecutor.

Public Prosecutor:

Your worship.

Judge President:

The floor is yours.

Public Prosecutor:

Your worship and dear audience. This court has received the complaint of Mr. Satan otherwise called Lucifer, who is here seated at the front bench. The scurrilous charges against God the creator that he has listed in his complaint

7

pushed us to go public today; this, in order to give him open opportunity to explain them in details and prove to the world what actually has been going on wrong between him and God.

Judge President:

That's fine. Proceed.

Public prosecutor:

Well, I may be wrong; but we the court; our perception however is that, these two guys, I mean God and Satan are partners in the creation of the world. I mean our world. Such being, us creatures have unfortunately been embroiled in their endless squabble, sometimes even losing our lives in the religious quagmire they have created. Actually, we don't know who is wrong and who is right between both. But, thanks to religious practices, we came to know about all this . . .

Satan:

Sorry, I have never created any religion or any church, mosque or whatever bull shit you call it. And I don't practice any religion at all. I am what I am and will never be want you want me to be.

Judge President:

Please, be quiet, Mr. Satan. Your opinion will be sought sometimes.

Satan:

I am sorry your worship. I wanted just to rectify a misunderstanding by human partisan mind.

Public Prosecutor:

Mr. Satan, please, stand up, go and get ready into the witness box. [*Satan rises and goes to stand inside the witness box*]

Judge President:

Proceed, Mr. Prosecutor.

Public prosecutor:

Thanks, your worship. [*Turning to Satan*]Also, the public has every reason to believe that, given the fact that Mr. Satan enjoys the status of the complainant; his statements will not be reckless, unethical and unsubstantiated. We don't need insults here. You are warned.

Satan:

Yes, Mr. Prosecutor. Call them allegations or whatever qualifications which please your intelligence; for me they are ingenious facts and that is that. I am not prepared to be intimidated by a court whose elements are already biased and who call my defamer "our creator". Allegedly, he is your creator. Not mine. [*The audience laugh. The Public Prosecutor looks at the Judge President, both amazed*]

Public Prosecutor:

Mr. Satan, Mr. Satan; please.

Satan :

Your worship.

Public Prosecutor:

Please, raise your right hand and swear to this court that you will tell only the truth and nothing else but the truth. [*Satan keeps quiet and stares at the Public Prosecutor without raising his hand; then looks at the audience.*] Mr. Satan. Mr. Satan.

Satan:

Yes, Mr. Public Prosecutor.

Public Prosecutor:

Please, raise your hand, I mean your right hand and take the oath to tell only the truth and nothing else than the truth to this court.

Satan:

There is no reason why I should raise my hand and swear to you. For, nobody among you here ignores me. The dead and the living, all know me. I am the truth itself; since your creation. There has not been any alteration in me ever since the world exists; be it physical or mental. None. Consequently, truth cannot swear to the truth. It would appear dichotomical and inner mostly conflictual. Just, let us say, it is stupid to ask the truth to swear to the truth. I, Satan; I am the truth.

[The audience laugh]

Public Prosecutor:

Mr. Satan; please, understand that it is the court procedure. And its relevance traduces the total commitment of the accused or the plaintiff to not deceive the court.

Satan:

You are used to me, all of you *[Pointing at the public]*. I have been living among you. I have never deceived anybody, because I am the one who has always been deceived by you and your alleged creator.

Judge President:

Ok. Leave it there and proceed, Mr. Prosecutor. *[Satan looks at the Judge President]*

Public prosecutor:

You are welcome your worship. For the good understanding of the public, it is worth reminding the background to this issue. Mr. Satan Lucifer was once in history dragged to a human court, after his arrest; a case which he brilliantly won though. And I commend him for that.

Satan:

You are more than welcome, your honour.

Public Prosecutor:

 Many years thereafter that historic trial, Mr. Satan decided to travel to heaven in order to defy father God and demand him___ clarifications concerning his allegations against him___Satan, and mostly the avalanche of calumnies thrown onto him by an army of so-called "men of God" who populate our planet and claim to work and speak on God's behalf.

Satan:

That's all right.

Public Prosecutor.

It seems, during that journey in heaven, an unknown planet which is situated millions miles away from reality; another battle occurred, out of which Mr. Satan and his team emerged victorious again. Today they are back and here among and with us . . .

Judge President:

Wait a bit. You say "his team"? Which team are you talking about?

Public Prosecutor:

Your worship, Mr. Satan made himself accompanied by a strong team of intellectual men. A team composed of his Excellency Karl Marx, His Majesty René Descartes, His modesty Jean-Paul Sartre, His highness Joseph Stalin and His Exceptional Jean Marie Arouet Voltaire. I don't know if these gentlemen are here? *[Trying to locate them in the court room]*

Crowd:

Yes, they are here.

Public Prosecutor:

Ok. I was saying, he was escorted by a think tank dream team. Messers René Descartes, Joseph Staline, Jean-Paul Sartre, Karl Marx and Voltaire. These guys gave a strong support to Mr. Satan's stance in challenging God about his pretentions to have solely created the whole world, and painstakingly, he exposed him to his celestial cabinet members that He-God failed to fulfil the promises he gave to the humanity of enjoying better life and living eternally.

Satan:

So far, that's perfect, your worship.

Public Prosecutor:

Thanks. Your worship, ladies and gentlemen, may I ask all the delegation members to stand up and come forth. [*They do rise up and proceed to the front bench.*]

Judge President:

They look smart. Please, gentlemen, return to your seats. Now, Mr. Satan Lucifer; what's the matter at this point in time?

Satan [*Looking at him silently]:*

You know you human beings; you seem to be minimising this case, each time I defend myself in your various houses of mind manipulation and corruption, that you call court houses or tribunals. *[The judge President looks at the Public Prosecutor with irritation].* All of you here suffer from amnesia. *[The judge President looks again at the Public Prosecutor, with amazement]*Besides, how do you want me to appear here without the presence of the accused? I don't want this one to be a monologue. My aim in coming to this court is to close this matter once and for all. You understand? That will henceforth put an end to speculations between me, you and God. Are you with me? For, when your presumed God and I Satan have to meet in public, it will be the end of religions and the collapse of churches' adventures on earth. Are you with me?

Judge President;

Yes, we are. Feed us more, Mr. Satan. Mr. Public Prosecutor.

Public Prosecutor:

Your worship.

Judge President:

Where is the accused? Where is God? Or shall we call him Mr, Ms or Mrs God. Where is God?

Public Prosecutor:

Your worship; maybe you have forgotten our last discussion. But, to the best memory of my knowledge, we spoke about this issue prior to registering this case for today's date. And it is because of the prolonged absence of God on Earth and the difficulty to locate him which has delayed this matter from early prosecution.

Judge President *[A bit disturbed]*

But, to my humble knowledge, God is omnipresent! How come that, we are served with a vanishing concept of a God that we never meet? Isn't it this a sheer illusion?

Public Prosecutor:

That is it, your worship. The court will proceed *in absentia.* However, we have some holy men and women here representing God and who promised to speak on his behalf.

Judge President:

Mr. Prosecutor, . . .

Public Prosecutor:

Your worship.

Judge President:

We don't want to conduct a serious hearing like the current one through proxies. God must come out here. I want him here, not a proxy person.

Public Prosecutor:

Your worship, you'll see the magic of God, let me tell you. One of these men here in long robes adorned with heavy crucifixes on their chests will incarnate God; and through him, He—God shall speak.

Satan:

Shall speak?

Public Prosecutor:

Certainly.

Judge President:

Damn it.

Satan:

I repeat it as well; I don't want fiction here, Mr. Prosecutor. I want facts. God. You see? I want him or her here. Whatever gender it is. It is a chance that I am offering him. For the sake of peace to the humanity, this rumour-mongering must end. I met him in camera few months ago. It was in heaven. But now, he must go public. I want him here.

Judge President: *[Ironising]*

Not only yourself, Mr. Satan. Even me, I want to see him. To touch him; even if it is once in my life; I may be saved as well. *[The gallery laughs]*

Satan:

You see. I am not the only one.

Public Prosecutor:

Thanks your worship. As man of law, I should admit that, I have been disturbed ever since this case landed in our hands.

Judge President:

How?

Public Prosecutor:

I spoke with Mr. Satan at great length, long before he filed for this confrontation with God___ the father. He refuses to be represented by a lawyer; rather, he preferred to be the plaintiff and the defence side himself at the same time. We really have a strong case here; so to speak. I am disturbed to the core.

Judge President:

Disturbed?

Public prosecutor:

Yes, your worship; I am. To tell the truth, I am.

Judge President:

Why?

Public Prosecutor:

It's an exceptional case that I am not used to; more particularly the way the plaintiff has formulated his complaint. It surpasses my judicial knowledge.

Judge President: [After *starring at him*]

I believe, Mr. Prosecutor, you've been trained for these matters. And, since I know you and have been working with you in this court, you have come across more difficult cases than this.

Public Prosecutor:

Indeed, your worship, we did encounter arduous cases in the history of this court. But, the current one is just . . . just . . . no match to the past cases.

Judge President:

You wouldn't envisage resigning from your duties Mr. Public Prosecutor?

Public Prosecutor:

No, I wouldn't. Your worship, I promise, I would not. But, suffer to hear that, I am grappling with it as regard how and where to start.

Judge President:

Given that, let us get started. Up to this point, we have already moved one step. Go ahead.

Public Prosecutor:

Your worship, the main plaintiff, Mr. Satan, has brought to this court, a lawsuit against God, the presumed creator of Earth and the whole Universe. He contends that, God, our creator, together with an army of religious earthly men, both God and those men have constituted a *cabale* of calumniators to defame him, to denigrate him and accuse him of all evils that affect our world. Allow me, your worship, and august audience, to warn everybody present in this court, that, this case shouldn't appear as a personal *vendetta* from Mr. Satan, but rather a legitimate lawsuit against God; the self-appointed creator and his representatives on our planet.

Judge President:

Hey, Mr. Satan. Before you continue, Mr. Public Prosecutor; can the dream team that accompanied Mr. Satan to meet God stand up again? I just want to familiarise myself with their faces.

[*They all stand up again, one by one.*]

Satan:

There they are. Oh! Look how smart these gentlemen are! [*Pointing at them.*]

22

Judge President:

Indeed, they are. Please, get seated, gentlemen. Mr. Public Prosecutor.

Public Prosecutor*: [Suddenly, enters a man dressed in a priest white outfit adorned with a big cross on his chest, and carrying a Bible.]*

And now, who is that gentleman?

[Everybody turns back to look at the new comer.]

Court Orderly:

Sorry, there is no place for you here. The court is fully packed. Can you wait outside?

Priest *(In white outfit)*:

I am the envoy of God. People of my congregation are in here too; and I am just joining them to defend our Lord. I am sorry for my late-coming, though.

Court Orderly *[Whispering to him]*:

The court proceedings have already started. So, stand still there.

Priest:

You can't defame Him like you plan. He is King of Kings.

Court Orderly:

Who? Who's the king you are talking about?

Priest:

The Almighty God____Me. He is in me.

Court Orderly: *[After smiling]*

That's fine. Get in now. But, it seems, the court wants God himself. Not proxies. Not intermediaries. And you must stop your *reverie* here. People come to talk sense in here. Not your usual platitudes that intoxicate and intimidate people everywhere and every time.

Priest:

But, but, but . . . I am the . . .

Judge President:

We don't want impostors and usurpers here. We need genuine individuals to defend their causes. Not ghosts. Not pretenders. Not impersonators. Understand? God himself is the one needed here. Not collaborators who speculate on everything without proving any tangible fact.

Priest:

My son, peace be upon you. [*He raises his cross and kisses it*] God will speak through me, through my colleagues here too. And there is no doubt about that, your worship. We are God's *impersonates*. As you see us, you have seen God.

Other clerical members in court:

Halleluiah. Praise the Most High.

Public prosecutor:

Ok. Just stand where you are. Perhaps we will need you sometimes. And you, the rest here; behave. This is neither a monastery nor a church...

Priest:

I am here at His Majesty's services; ready to answer your questions. I am divinely inspired; and I am Him talking.

Other clerical members in court:

Halleluiah! Praise the Lord.

Judge President:

Listen; ladies and gentlemen; we conduct the State's serious business in here. It's not a choir...

Priest:

We do understand; your worship.

Public Prosecutor:

Then, do you mind standing in the accused box, Mr. Impostor?

Priest:

Sure. For our Lord, we will die. We will do anything possible at our disposal to defend The Most High. He is with us here. His gracious holy spirit and magnitude also umbrella us. Praised be his name. The Most High. Oh Jesus! The living one who defeated death.

Judge President: *[Hammering on the table]*

Stop that incantation here. It's just irritating. *[Hammering the table again]*

Priest:

Your worship. I . . . .

Judge President: *[Pointing at the priest]*

Promise me that you would not preach in this court house. For, we won't allow those hilarious deviations in here. We've had pretty enough with these void preachings ever since the world exists.

Priest:

Be blessed, my son, in the name of Jesus, the Most High and be anointed by the oil of His Majesty God; the omnipotent, omnipresent and the omniscient one.

Judge President *[A bit irate]***:**

Police man . . .

Court Orderly:

Your worship.

Judge President:

There is something wrong with that man. Watch him. For, this is not a church; and I dislike such predicaments in such places.

Court Orderly: *[Approaching the priest and looking sternly into his eyes.]*

Have you heard? *[Pointing his finger on his face]* One word again and I walk you out of here. One. So, zip your mouth and wait until you are needed to speak.

Priest:

My apology; my son.

Court Orderly:

It's accepted. But mark my word.

Satan:

Watch out for false prophets. They come to you in sheep's clothing, but inwardly they are ferocious wolves, says their book of Matthew 7:15.

Priest: *[To the Judge President]*

My son, you will not challenge a man of God, for he always brings good tidings. It's not that I am bad as you think.

Judge President:

Sir, you have firmly promised that you wouldn't disrupt the court proceedings.

Priest:

Pardon me, my son. The divine syndrome in me keeps me talking.

Satan:

Mr. President, let me quote some passages from the book this man is holding *[Pointing at the priest.]*

Jemadari Vi-Bee-Kil Kilele

Judge President:

Yes, go ahead.

Satan:

Thanks your worship.

Matthew says this at (24:11)," *and many false prophets will appear and deceive many people. I have not sent him,* declares their Lord. *They are prophesying lies in my name. Therefore, I will banish you and you will perish both you and the prophets who prophesy to you.*" You read this again in Jeremiah 27:15, Acts 20:29:20, and also in 2 Peter 2:1:3. So, in your conducting these proceedings, be aware of those facts. Mr. President.

Judge President:

Thanks for highlighting those passages to this court, Mr. Satan. They are sign posts and we promise to be cautious. Mr. Public prosecutor, you have the floor.

Public Prosecutor:

Thanks your worship. Mr. Satan. Many people, curious to see you for their first time, would love to know, what brings you here? We already have exposed some elements of what you may say in addition. Any exceptional report from the trip you made to heaven?

Satan:

Oh yeah! There is. 'f course there is. There is a lot to be exposed in order to rectify the truth-lie you human beings have been officially told and to which you are used. A lot.

Public Prosecutor:

You have the floor, Mr. Satan Lucifer.

Satan:

Thanks your worship. First of all, I have to thank my supporters here, human beings like you, who, frankly speaking have dared challenge all the bullshit of religious teachings instilled in you from one generation to another. It means, honestly speaking, I haven't been alone in the struggle. You see?

Public Prosecutor:

We are listening.

Satan:

These gentlemen are superb and deserve to be decorated with the Order of Doubt and Rejection, for having helped crash God's pretentions. The overwhelming support to my stand by these gentlemen has just shown how men and a defamed character like me, can work hand in hand to eradicate lies and instil respect into our diversity and live in peace and harmony, without interference of hypocrite people like God, over wise called Baphomet goat, the Holy Shit, Jesus Crook and his army of preachers,___ them who sponsor conflicts and ignite wars all over the world.

Public Prosecutor:

That's right. Go ahead.

Satan:

These gentlemen have accompanied me to heaven and witnessed the encounter between me and God.

Judge President: [*He chuckles a bit*]

Did you really meet God?

Satan:

Yes, I did. And we do meet quite often. *[Smiling]*

Public Prosecutor:

Really?

Satan:

Gosh! What do you think?

Public Prosecutor:

Nothing. We just want a confirmation!

Satan:

What you learn between me and him is really a surprise to me; but we are so closely connected to each other. The rest of so-called feud between me and God is a movie version for public consumption. The real story, as always, is different from the official literature disseminated amongst you.

Judge President:

How does he look like? [*The public gallery laughs*]

Satan:

I brought a picture of the occasion for you. Here it is [*Showing it out*].

Judge President:

Mr. Prosecutor.

Public Prosecutor:

Your worship.

Judge President:

Can you just bring it closer to me? [*After observing it*] It's splendid.

Satan:

Thank you. We are old buddies; me and your so-called God. We do meet and do many things together without your knowing. On your side, forget about those religious and speculative statements that confirm that God has given me a limited period of life time, after which he will kill me. That will never happen. I am not a genre to be intimidated. I am as immortal as he is.

Public Prosecutor:

Go ahead. We'd love to hear more.

Satan:

Ladies and Gentlemen; God that you praise and worship is a fearful tyrant and despot akin to those who rule you here on Earth. The likes of Genkis Khan, Napoleon, Mobutu Sese Seko, Jean Bedel Bokasa, Jean-Claude Duvalier, Ferdinand Marcos, Nicholaeu Ceascescu, Joseph Kabila, Adolf Hitler, Pinochet, Apartheid rulers, Kamuzu Banda, Paul Kagame and Idi Amin Dada. That's what he is. He always imposes his opinion and wouldn't let you insert any new thought between his pronouncements. You see?

Judge President:

Illustrate your accusation Mr. Satan, by evidencing elements of that dictatorship. You can't be sulking.

Satan:

Sure. Let us start with this court for example.

Public prosecutor:

Yes. We're listening. What is wrong with this court, Mr. Satan?

Satan:

Please, hold your breath.

You read in Psalms 139:7-10, Ephesians 1:23, Matthew 6:8, 1 John 3:20, Luke 16:15, Psalms 139:4 and Romans 16:27; 11:33, all in the Bible; that, God is omnipotent, omniscient and omnipresent. Isn't it?

The Gallery:

Hmmmmmmm!

Satan:

Now, where is he in here? Even the Judge President wants to see him? But where is he? Where is God? That's the first lie. Dictators are sick-liars. And, he is one of them; that guy you all call God. He imposes the credo that he is everywhere, yet he is AOL!

Public Prosecutor:

Yeah! But . . . but, I want you to tell this court more about your trip to Heaven, Mr. Satan. And why God should be brought before this court. I am talking from a Christian point of view.

Satan:

You are not a Christian. Rather, you are Christianised.

Public Prosecutor:

Meaning?

Satan:

That means, Christianity has been imposed onto you. To be exact, it's a punishment to you; pure slavery!

Public Prosecutor [*He stares at the Judge President]:*

Well, let it be.

Satan:

In front of these gentlemen, René Descartes, Joseph Stalin, Karl Marx, Voltaire, Jean-Paul Sartre and few members of his celestial cabinet, I challenged God that all his millennial allegations against me were false.

Judge President:

How possible?

Satan:

Ask them. *[Pointing at his dream team]*Truly, God admitted to his failure to meeting human expectations and aspirations to happiness and better material life.

Public Prosecutor:

But, God is not obliged to ameliorate our lives. From my Christian point of view, I believe he has done enough. And it is up to everyone to fend for one's life.

Satan:

As a matter of fact, it is not what has been happening. One wonders why many of you people play the hypocrite game with your own lives! You've been suffering pretty much. For too long: starvation, wars, natural catastrophes, racial injustices, crippled government finance ministries, etc . . . It contradicts all his honey promises.

Priest:

Don't exaggerate.

[Satan stops for a while, looking at him, then . . .]

Satan:

For example, this much publicized and hypothetical coming of Jesus crank; will he really come back? When? Can't you people, at once adjust your mind for a while and give sense to your existence as reasonable animals?

Public Prosecutor:

We are doing that; but none can challenge God's promises.

Priest:

Surely. Our Lord is coming.

Satan:

"Jesus will come, Jesus will come." What a hoax! Besides, he will come to do what? What has he forgotten here in the first place that he wants to come to recuperate? To humble knowledge, he had had ample time to pack up and go!

Priest:

None of God's promises has failed. You are just a blackmailer. An ungrateful, an . . .

Satan:

I think, he is the one who deserves to be called blackmailer. These poor people here have been praying, believing in him, worshiping him, dancing and singing for him, but the reward and award they get in return is only suffering; coupled with death. How is it that all your God's promises are always conditional? Have not you met those conditions yet ever since you exist? If at all you do exist.

Priest:

Human beings must always please God. It is a must. And there is a prize in the end.

Satan:

You see. Such a selfish God. He only wants to be praised and be given, but not to give back; instead, he curses [*Genesis 3:16-17*] and threatens people daily. The whole world is frustrated because of an imminent cataclysmic end that his accomplices call Armageddon. Other sick mind even talk about the 2012 doom, the Mayan calendar, etc…

Judge President:

Ok. Can you go back to your encounter with God? Because much of what you are saying now sounds personal between God and you. They do not concern today's court proceedings.

Satan:

Thanks, your worship. God also recognized publicly that, I, Lucifer was not a rebel angel as you are told. Upon creating you, as you read it in Genesis 1:26; among all gods who participated in your moulding, I wanted to know more and load you with higher intelligence that would liberate you from the daily bondage of needs and wants, and just live eternal life like us gods. But he, Yahweh wanted to keep you in ignorance and parasitism so that you could be relying on his misty promises. Read it in Genesis 2:17 and in Genesis 3:7; because, there is no God, but there are gods. Read it in genesis 1:26.

Judge President:

What a blasphemy?

Public Prosecutor:

Say it again your worship.

Satan: *[After starring at the Public Prosecutor]*

What! Listen carefully, all of you here in this hall of shame. For having thought of you, I was dubbed Prince of evil. But, I am the guy to be worshipped instead. I have been fighting for you since the world exists. Because, I really interfered with the experiment we conducted on Earth as a group of scientists.

Judge President:

Really?

Satan:

Oh yeah! Among all gods who participated in the creation process, I was the only one who wanted you to have a larger brain capacity that could help you think for yourselves instead of being tied up to a rope of belief in a certain almighty God. For my struggle to free you, me and Yahweh became enemies.

Public Prosecutor:

This is an amazing lecture you are giving. Carry on Mr. Satan.

Satan:

Had they allowed me to pursue my attempt to alter you, your greater brain capacity would have created a sort of quantum leap to surpass ours or else to match it. Reason why I am always tarnished by Yahweh and his accomplices.

Public Prosecutor:

It's pretty strange.

Satan:

Read it in the book of Genesis 3:9-15. Yahweh anticipated everything to go into his favour. Today I am the planet's *baddest* guy.

Public prosecutor.

Who are the "We" that you have just mentioned?

Satan:

Me___ Lucifer, Yahweh and many other gods. Learn that we the gods are a population just like you; but unlike you, we are a minority and indeed, immortals. Only a god can kill another god. [*The public Prosecutor looks at the Judge*

President] I know that you are not much cognizant of that old guy called Yahweh who is a spiritual reality like me. You only praise him; but us, we take him as a colleague. We are of an *etheric* race called the *Elohim*. The god-creators. Read it in the book of Genesis 6: 1-4.

Judge President:

For verification sake, we shall do as you recommend Mr. Satan, right?

Satan:

All right sir. Tell me, by reading that book called Bible, do you make an effort to understand its passages or you; you just cram it or swallow its contents unquestioningly like a baby would swallow a bottle of milk?

Public Prosecutor:

I think that does not have anything to do with you here. Does anyone have a Bible here?

Priest: *[Rushing]*

I do. I do have one. Because this is our weapon against speculators like this man. He is just a dangerous and professional liar.[*Satan looks at him speechlessly]*

Judge President:

You promised that you would not compromise these proceedings with finger pointing. Please, take your stand and do not insult people here. This is a State premises. Consequently one's got to behave like a good Earth citizen.

Priest:

My apologies, your worship.

Judge President:

You are welcome. Please, carry on.

Priest:

Thanks your worship. The quote in the book of Genesis says this:

"And it came to pass, when men began to multiply upon the face of the earth, and daughters were born unto them. The sons of God(Elohim) saw daughters of men that they were fair; and they took unto them wives of all which they chose . . . There were giants in the earth in those days; and also that when the sons of God(Elohim) came in unto the

daughters of men, and they bare children of them, the same became mighty men of old, men of renown."

Other clerical members in court:

Amen.

Judge President*[Turning towards Satan]:*

So?

Satan:

You find the same stark reality referring to us Elohim in 1 Samuel 28:13, genesis 1:26, Genesis 20:13. We also are known as Nephilims.

Judge President:

Who are the Elohims or Nephilims or else Seraphims you're talking about??

Satan:

Elohims or Nephilims are us god-creators of which reference is made in your book of manipulation. It is us who created you. I and Yahweh were part of the process, together with other gods whose names he does not want to mention in the Bible. He rather portrays us as a plague to be done away with. Truly this is not fair at all. It's not serious.

Judge President:

And then, what went wrong then?

Satan:

I don't like the monarchic way Mr. Yahweh adopted to behave.

Public Prosecutor:

Which one? Which way?

Satan:

Of grabbing all the intellectual property of creation and proclaiming himself Almighty. That, dear human beings, I can't take. I have been keeping mum for too long. But of now, all the taboos and arcanes I was forced to trove must be revealed to everyone.

Public Prosecutor:

You must find a way to reconcile with him, mostly by humbling yourself. He is a loving father, always ready to pardon everyone and everything wrongly done. *[Satan stares at him, nods, then laughs]*

Satan:

You don't seem to understand anything at all. And yet, in Genesis 1:26, he said, *"Let us make man in our image, according to our likeness."*

Public Persecutor:

I like that part. *[Satan turns and stares at him again]*

Satan:

Had he been alone during that creation experiment, why couldn't he say *"Let me make . . ."* By that virtue, why do you want me to kneel down to him, yet we are equal? *[The whole court is flabbergasted]*

Judge President:

Anyway, it was just an advice from us. But, but where are other gods you are talking about?

Satan:

They are around you.

Judge President:

Around us! Where?

Satan:

In your houses, and wherever you go; spirits watch you.

Public Prosecutor:

Like satellites.

Satan:

Listen, each race was represented by an Elohim. Me I am the black race Elohim; but, I am not a racist. When creating human being, each Elohim contributed scientifically to the process. Just like a team of builders; each workman brings a stone, a brick, etc . . . to build a house. And after, we would say, this house is yours, that house belongs to him, etc.

Public Prosecutor:

But, as you say, what proves that you are god of the Black race?

Satan:

Primarily, yes. I am the one. Because, I rule over the whole Earth planet. Reason why Yahweh can't easily come here unless our Immigration services accord him a visa. Secondarily, I am always painted as black *[laughter from the audience]*

Judge President:

We would like to learn more about this perpetual conflict between you and God, more especially from your side of story. But, again let us put things straight, Mr. Satan. Are you here to criticise the Bible, I mean to accuse the Bible, Jesus Christ or God?

Satan:

All three. Because all make one. Nobody would know about this god without the Bible or any other so-called holy shit book. And nobody would know the Bible without this fiction of god and this tragic drama of Jesus-Christ. So, my grievance is directed on to all.

Judge President:

Anyway, that is how you consider those tree entities. But, let us get more about the rationale of your accusation against God.

Satan:

I am here again to defend our race___the black race. To justify this, refer to the book of Genesis again 9:20-21. The curse of Ham's Canaan by Noah. So, us Blacks, we were cursed by this drunken vine farmer who left himself naked after imbibing a great dose of wine? I, Satan, too am a black man, because they always paint me black; as I said.

Judge President:

We're not here to discuss racial slurs and stereotypes, sir. This court has its racial integrity and rational ethics.

Satan:

I do understand

Judge President:

Consequently, we will not entertain any racial prejudice neither will we allow the deviation from the matters lodged into your complaint to this court, Mr. Satan.

Satan:

Listen, your worship. I have been the victim of God and you people who always paint me black; and that I do accept now and I am ready to fight you as a black man. You've never portrayed me as of your favourite colours: white, yellow or red, which are your pet racial colours. Consequently, my rejection of your religions which have sabotaged our negro-African culture is starting.

Public Prosecutor:

We will tackle those allegations at a later stage, Mr. Satan. But . . . but . . .

Satan:

I am so sorry Mr. Public Prosecutor. Read that Bible on Deuteronomy 13:6-10 and tell me what is what.

Judge President:

All right. For peace sake, can someone read that passage? Mr. God or rather representative of God. Please, read out for the audience.

Priest:

Blessed you are, your worship. *[He Kisses the Bible]*The book of Deuteronomy, which is the 5th book in the line of The Old Testament within the holy Bible, says this: Deuteronomy 13:6-10.

"If a prophet, or one who foretells by dreams, appears among you and announces to you a miraculous sign or wonder, and if the sign or wonder of which he has spoken takes place, and he says, "Let us follow other gods" (gods you have not known) 'and let us worship them," you must not listen to the words of that prophet or dreamer . . . . That prophet or dreamer must be put to death, because he preached rebellion against the LORD your God, ..."

[The Priest starts trembling]

Satan:

Yes, yes, that is it. Continue up to verse 11, mostly read verse 9 to 10 which are the clincher ones.

Priest:

Ok, be calm. Don't pull me like a farm cart. I am reading everything you want, in the name of the Lord, because this is his holy word. Let us continue. *"Do not spare him or shield him. You must certainly put him to death. [He shrieks loudly, and then keeps on shivering] Your hand must be the first in putting him to death, and then the hands of all the people. Stone him to death, because he tried to turn you away from the Lord your God . . . ."*

[The public seems agitated]

Court orderly:

Silence . . . Silence.

Public Prosecutor:

And what is your stance in there, Mr. Satan?

Satan:

It's clear. Can't you see? The passage tells it all. You see? Us Africans, we have our gods. Me being one of them. But the colonial church and its preachers, like this one; for more than five centuries have worked hard to deviate us from our local gods in order to worship theirs, more particularly this drunken god of Israel. The same god instructs that we must stone and kill all the priests and preachers. That's fine. However, he is advocating terrorism. Nonetheless, I support his opinion. We must kill everybody who comes to our African villages to spread the lies of this dictatorial Yahweh. So, let us start with this one.

Public gallery:

He is right, he is right, he is right. *[The public stands up, shouting, baying for the Priest's blood. A pandemonium reigns inside the court room.]*

Court Orderly:

Silence, silence in the court. *[Losing his temper; he pulls his gun from the holster, and aims it at the public.]* One will lose one's life here if you don't shut your fucken mouths. Shut up. *[Loudly]*

Judge President: *[Hammering on the table]*

Shut up everybody. Shut up. *[After a while, the public gallery cools down, and the proceedings resume]*

Public Prosecutor:

Oh! My God! That was terrible! Thanks Mr. Officer. *[Looking up to the Priest]* Any reaction, your reverence? And you said, the Almighty God would speak through you.

Priest:

There is no doubt about it. He is the one talking now. The holy word. Word of salvation, my child. World of life.

Satan:*[Pointing finger at the priest]*

We will stone you to death. *Farceur.* And we will ask for compensation for damages caused of having geared us from our local gods to foreign gods, for more than 500 years.

Public Gallery:

Yes, yes, yes, yes . . . .

Judge President*: [Hammering the table]*

Silence. Silence in the court.

Court Orderly:

Keep quiet, Keep quiet . . .

Judge President *[Murmuring to his two assessors.]:*

It looks like Satan's rising.

First Assessor:

Indeed, it does. Satan's beginning to rise.

Second Assessor:

It stinks a looming danger.

Judge President:

Don't worry. We shall manage whatever will happen.
[Turning to Satan]

Pay attention Mr. Satan; and you too, the public. This court
may indict you again for incitement to violence. Don't add
case on cases. The *dénouement* may take long to unfold.
Understand?

Satan:

I am sorry your worship. But Yawheh_God and his army of preachers owe us a lot. Consequently, I can't continue to apologise for misconduct in this court.

Judge President:

The court will help you to recuperate your lost cultural property and pride, even the reparation to your dignity as you allege.

Satan:

I am not alleging, your worship. I am confirming. And I repeat, I am asserting that, this god and his accomplices of preachers ought to be punished. Look at this fact, your worship.

Judge President:

Yes. Which one?

Satan:

When an African healer heals sick people by laying his hands on the patient or when he falls into trance to receive ancestral powers to heal, these people called "men of God" label that, *witchcraft, sorcery, charlatanism*. But today, when all the pastors and preachers do that, it is called divine miracle. Just watch all religious TV channels. You find that normal?

[The public gallery clap hands]

Public Prosecutor:

Surely, what you say makes sense. Mr. Satan. Please, go ahead.

Satan:

When Jesus Christ rises up in Israel to demand the independence of his country, fighting against Roman colonisation, occupation and dominance, they call it word of God; but when our African heroes, the likes of Patrice Lumumba, Nkwame Nkrumah, Steve Biko, Kimpa Vita, Nelson Mandela, Simon Kimbangu, Sekou Touré, Samory Touré, Robert Mugabe, etc. do the same, they are labelled communists, terrorists, dictators, revolutionaries, Satanists. Do you find that normal?

[The public gallery clap hands again]

Priest: [*Now impersonating God. He changes his tone*]

I am your master, your creator. You cannot rebel against me. You cannot serve two masters at a time, my son. I love you and you must understand that only love should prevail in everything. Love your brother man. Nothing but love.

Satan:

Your worship. These people keep on preaching to us about peace, love and asking us to cram all their insanities from these albums of lies they dub "*Holy this and holy that*"; while they arm themselves with guns and all sorts of weapons of mass destruction, killing people everywhere and every day. How holy is that word?

Priest:

Death, my son, is a temporary punishment. You should not fear it. I just put you to sleep for a while. It is a little spanking to bring you close to me, as you tend to disrespect me.

Public Prosecutor:

Mr. Satan, did you meet Jesus Christ in Heaven during your trip to there?

Satan:

(Laughing) It is nothing but a lie. I and my friends over there, we never heard of that guy there. God pretended that, prior to our arrival; Jesus went on an errand in the vicinities, a statement which was not true. Because, our stay lasted almost three days in there and there was no sign of Jesus Christ.

René Descartes:

Frankly speaking, God is alone up there; but surrounded by some sycophants that he calls Ministers. A bunch of feet-leakers who chant and dance to his tune of dictatorship.

Priest:

Soon, Jesus will come down, my son.

Joseph Stalin:

To do what?

Priest:

To bring peace on to the earth. To kill dictators like you and to take over all the governments of the world.

Public prosecutor:

Yes, do you mind repeating what you have just said, dear father?

Priest:

Of course, your worship; Jesus is coming very soon, to make real justice system reign supreme and replace this human comedy.

Public Prosecutor: *[A bit hurt]*

Won't he need us to work in his government?

Priest:

He needs nobody. No human assistance; for you are of a perverted and untrustworthy race. His Majesty once spoke of race of vipers. *[The public Prosecutor looks up at the Judge President]*

René Descartes:

But, you and all the troops of priests here in this court room as well as in the world wide claim to be assisting him.

Priest:

That's holy and perfect, my son.

René Descartes:

So, you are what is written in Romans 16:17-18 that "*I urge you, brothers, to watch out for those who cause divisions and put obstacles in your way that are contrary to the teaching you have learned. Keep away from them. For such people are not serving our Lord Christ, but their own appetites.*"

[The Priest keeps on shivering and exclaiming, by rolling out his eyeballs]

Voltaire:

Furthermore, in 2 Corinthians 11:13-15; it is even clearly mentioned that: "For *such men are false apostles, deceitful workmen, masquerading as apostles of Christ. And no wonder, for Satan himself masquerades as an angel of light. It is not surprising, then, if his servants masquerade as servants of righteousness. Their end will be what their actions deserve.*"

Priest:

Ah! You hear that? The end of you who are his servants will be disastrous.

Voltaire:

That will never happen. And we cannot panic because of that void threat; because, Mr. Satan is strong and all of you are afraid of him. One wonders why a full army of calumniators has been unable to defeat a lone man. What wrong has he done to you?

Priest:

He is disobedient. And soon Jesus Christ is coming to read the final verdict of his end.

Joseph Stalin:

That means, Jesus Christ went away to study politics and law. And now, he is returning to make a historic bloody *coup d'état*, to kill all of us and proclaim himself President of this world? That is terrorism coupled with dictatorship. Nothing else.

Judge President:

Ladies and gentlemen; this court has recorded all the statements of Mr. Satan together with his team mates; statements that we wish God or rather his representative here present will have to answer when we return tomorrow. [*He stands up*]

Court Orderly:

All rise.

[*Everybody rises. Exit Judge President. The gallery resumes its menace on the Priest*]

ACT II: SCENE 1

[The court proceedings resume one day after]

Public Prosecutor: *[After a silent prayer]*

I wish today's judgement be put under the prescriptions of the holy book of Mathew 7:1 which says *"Do not judge, or you too will be judged. For in the same way as you judge others, you will be judged, and with the measure you use, it will be measured to you."* Mr Satan.

Satan:

Your worship. I have been judged many times. Even now, despite my law suit, it is obvious I am the one being judged here now. But, I am not afraid of that. You should know by now that I am used to unfounded accusations.

Public Prosecutor:

I don't think so. You are the plaintiff. That's all I know. Mr. Satan, one day ago, you spoke about God and his son, Jesus-Christ. Indeed you accused God of being racist and divisive. Can you, just elaborate on that, if you do not mind?

Satan:

Thanks, your worship and dear audience. One day, a Canaanite woman from the vicinity came to Jesus, hysterically crying out so that Jesus could go to heal her daughter who was suffering terribly from demon-possession.

Public Prosecutor:

Is it?

Satan:

Oh yeah! And all that is accusation against me___the Demon. *[Pointing to his chest]* You see? Tell you what. Jesus refused even to listen to the poor woman.

Judge President:

Why?

Satan:

Because she was black. [*The Judge President stares at the Public Prosecutor*] She was my sister. Besides, he racially responded this to the desperate woman. Listen to this:" *I was sent only to the lost sheep of Israel.*" Read it in Matthew 15:22-24.

Voltaire:

Allow me to add that Jesus' statement is a hate speech.

Karl Marx:

Oh yeah; it is. Such teaching is even discriminatory and sectarian; awful indeed. And it reaches its climax when Jesus-Christ himself sends his 12 disciples out with the following instructions: "*Do not go among the Gentiles or enter any town of the Samaritans. Go rather to the lost sheep of Israel.*" Read it in Matthew 10:5-6

Judge President:

And then? What . . . .

Karl Marx:

Meaning that, your Jesus did not come for any other human race or tribe, save his country and his countrymen.

Judge President:

You don't give Jesus a chance at all?

Stalin:

Ah no. Jesus' mind set was discriminatory.

Jean-Paul Sartre:

Your worship. Now you can see the light; that, the one you label "*Saviour of the humanity*" is just a racist, a tribalistic character whose mission limits itself to a certain region. And given such harsh words from the supposed saviour of the humanity, the poor black woman continued to implore him so that he could help; rather, he brutally and arrogantly got angry and insulted that black woman in the following manner: "*It is not right to take the children's bread and toss it to the dogs.*"

Judge President: *[Rising up from the seat]*

What?

Satan:

Your worship; read it in Mathew 15:26, and in Mathew 27:11. So, this god and his so-called son are not of ours and should stop invading our countries, because, clearly speaking they were not sent for us. And they regard us Blacks as and other races as *"dogs."*

Judge President:

I sympathize with you Mr. Satan. But, to my humble knowledge, many people who are not Jesus' country men feel comfortable about him and their Christianity has produced wonders into their lives. Why are you so against Christianity? Why are you so incensed with God, I mean our father who is in heaven? *[Ironising]*

Satan:

Your worship, I am not against it. I am just putting things straight. You see? The anti-Christs are those who teach the contrary of what their Jesus said. The Bible says, Jesus was not sent for anybody else, save the Israelites. But, a bunch of conspirators and money-mongers contradict Jesus' statements and keep on imposing on us their divine illusions. Voltaire has just referred you to 2 Corinthians 11:13-15. Who then is the anti-Christ?

Judge President:

But even the Israelites themselves; they rejected Jesus-Christ that he is not their saviour!

Public Prosecutor

And they keep on waiting for another one, yet to come.

Satan: *[After a pause]*

But that is not enough. For, there has been, for too long a huge and endless black mail about the alleged death of Jesus-Christ. That, he died for us. He suffered for us. He sheded his blood for us; and this and that.

Priest:

Indeed, His Majesty Lord Jesus-Christ died the most atrocious death. It is undeniable, my son.

Public Prosecutor:

That is true. *[Faintly]*

Satan:

But, who asked him to die? We never called him to face the death. Those who killed him are not of ours; and he died in a strange land; which is not ours. How sadder is his passing compared with that of the many that perish in war conflicts?

Priest:

His Majesty was born a universal man and he died for the entire universe; because he created the universe. So, there is no black mail in asking people to pray and worship His Majesty. It is the only way to redeem them.

Judge President:

It seems, by killing Jesus-Christ, human beings did something very wrong. So, the only way to wash away that awful transgression is by bringing the whole entire humanity very close to God, through scriptures teachings and learning. And you Mr. Satan, being one of this world has no choice if not doing what the majority does.

Satan:

Do you mean, your worship that the whole world has hijacked a philosophy which is not theirs?

Judge President:

It looks like. But a lucrative philosophy, though. Merely, it is an imposition, not a free conversion to a certain faith.

Satan:

Yeah; it is a mega business. Mark that the real dictatorship starts and remains inside those "houses of Gods."

Public Prosecutor:

To my best knowledge, conversion to a certain faith is equal to a persuasion.

Satan:

Perfect. But, Jesus and his so-called father are a duet of impostors. Beside, how can God be called *father,* yet he is not married? Me, I am as godly as single as him; yet nobody calls me *father.* Why?

Public Prosecutor:

Perhaps you would not feel comfortable with such appellation. Nevertheless, there are many unmarried fathers out there. While we respect the institution called marriage, such does not stop some people from enjoying the status of fatherhood, though.

Satan:

You mean, your god is a human being? Who then is his wife?

Public Prosecutor:

Well, I am not a biologist, but I think, God can be a hermaphrodite.

Satan:

So, being bisexual he can give birth to kids? Particularly hybrid kids?

Public Prosecutor:

You mean?

Satan:

But, human beings do not know Jesus' gender. Was he a man or a woman?

Judge President:

A powerful man who died for you. Jesus remains phenomenal despite all your slurs, Mr. Satan.

Satan:

I don't care his successes. It is all a lie. Your worship; read it in Matthew 27:36-37, Matthew 27:11 and Matthew 27:28-29. Therefore, Jesus died for his fellow men of Israel not for us Negro-Africans. I am not an Israelite. Must I repeat it?

Public Prosecutor:

Mr. Satan, you are such an impressive and avid Bible reader. One just gets amazed about the precision of references that you supply each time you speak; you know.

Satan:

You can't be amazed, your worship. I know the Bible contents. I participated to its drafting. But human beings spiced it with their own stories in order to enslave other people and take advantage of their naivety in a bid to plunder their resources and cage them in perpetual and unsuspected mental bondage.

Priest:

How do you substantiate all these speculations, Mr. Devil? You well know that the Bible is my words. It's the word of God.

Satan:

May you please shut up? You call this your word? A book full of contradictions and atrocities?

Priest:

This is not a place to settle record, Mr. Satan.

Satan:

I have given a great chance to Yahweh to settle this case out of court. Long, long time ago. But he persisted in deploying and redeploying his army of deceivers to tarnish my image.

Judge President:

In order to allow us finish this case smoothly, I call for calm between you too.

Satan:

I never killed anybody, me Satan, but Yahweh has been killing people ever since this world exists; and he boasts about it in the Bible. You remember Sodom and Gomorrah and many other mass murders. Never has my name been linked to those atrocities. So why have you been tarnishing my image? *[Pointing at Priest]*

Priest:

May we meet after this?

Satan:

Listen, I don't need that. I saw you human beings re-drafting this mop of lies in Turkey in order to go out there and invade further territories, preaching poisonous gospel to unaware populations, simply because you envy other people's resources.

Priest:

Listen . . .

Satan:

Colonialists claim that Jesus sent them to recruit disciples and go out there to convert heathens. That's a damaging allegation. But, I know, Jesus never said that. It's a falsification of history. We Africans are not heathens and we do not need conversion to a criminals' faith that you call civilisation.

[Holding an open Bible, the priest raises his finger, asking for permission to read the Bible]

Public Prosecutor:

Yes, my father. You may read for the court.

Priest:

Here is a proof that our Lord Jesus Christ is king of kings. Listen carefully. Above his head they placed the written charge against him:" *THIS IS JESUS, THE KING OF THE JEWS.*"

Satan:

Of course; not of Africans!

Priest:

Wait.

Satan:

So, what else do you have to say? The man called Jesus was the presumed king of the Jews. Why then, do you keep on imposing on other people a king who is not theirs? And, besides, Israel never was a kingdom.

Priest:

Come back to the house, prodigal son. Come, come.

Satan:

You never showed me my mother! So, how can I be called a son of somebody?

[Jean-Paul Sartre raises his hand]

Judge President:

Yes, gentleman. Do you have anything new to add?

Jean-Paul Sartre:

Yes, I do. I have a question to ask. Once in his life-span, Jesus felt that he was going to fail in his mission to help liberate Israel out of the grip of Romans; he decided one night to go and consult spirits of his ancestors at a cemetery. That night, he took with him, three disciples: Peter, John and James. And that, he had private and long talk with Moses and Elijah [Refer to Luke 9:28-30]. But, if an African man goes to cemetery to consult the spirit of his ancestors, quickly he is labelled "wizard, sorcerer, witch, etc . . ." How much difference is there, between Jesus who consults the fathers of Israeli independence and an African person who does the same?

Priest:

Jesus liked to pray at Gethsemane. It was a holy garden; a hideout for serene meditation.

Satan:

Thanks for lending me a hand; Sartre. Yes, read it in Matthew 26:30-45. Of course, it was a cemetery; full of skulls and many bones of dead people.

Priest: *[After starring at him]*

You must respect God . . . for, he is your father.

Satan:

He is not my God. Because, himself on Exodus 3:1-2, he says this to Moses." *I am the God of your father, the God of Abraham, the God of Isaac and the God of Jacob.*" He is clear, that God. What more can I say?

René Descartes:

On that point, your worship, allow me to clarify one thing. I mean one confusion.

Judge President:

Which one, Mr. Descartes?

Descartes:

I am directing my question to this pretentious father; Oh sorry, God's medium.

Judge President:

Yes, go ahead.

Descartes:

Thanks, your worship. First of all, at mount Horeb, while grazing the cattle of his father-in law, Jethro, did Moses speak to God or to an angel?

Priest:

He spoke to God. The real God of Israel who appeared to him in the form of thunder ball fire. You see. Besides, just like Moses; you can't see God. If you see him you die. You die. You see?

[Stalin nods in disapproval]

Descartes:

But in Exodus 3:1-2, it is said "*the angel of God appeared to Moses*". An angel; and not God. That angel told Moses . . .; "*I am the god of Abraham, the god of Isaac, and the god of Jacob.*" You see, in the first verse, we have seen that Moses has seen an angel. Yet, in the following verse, the same angel affirms to Moses that he is the god of Abraham, the god of Isaac, the god of Jacob. The same Jacob who also is called Israel. May we, at this point in time and collectively here agree that the angel who appeared to Moses at mount Horeb was called Israel Jacob Yahweh and that, it was not God?

Priest:

It is God who Abraham saw. The real God. You know God can take different shapes!

Public Prosecutor:

Which God?

Priest:

The Almighty God of Israel. Your God too.

Karl Marx:

But in Exodus, 3:16-17, it is once more said to Moses the following: *"Go, assemble the elders of Israel and say to them, The Lord, the God of your fathers_____the God of Abraham, Isaac and Jacob____appeared to me . . . ."*. So, it is their god and nobody else's.

Priest

You are human beings. As long as you don't have guidance from the Holy Spirit, you cannot comprehend God's words. It's a mystery.

Voltaire:

I would even say, that you are guilty and dictatorial for having, for many years brainwashed people to worship your god, a foreign god and destroying over people's basis of their national culture and traditional values.

Satan:

Your worship; there are loads of unmet promises that this god made to us and that he never materialized. I wonder why he should continue to be called father, he who has dismally failed in his mission as the whole thing provider.

Judge President:

Ladies and gentlemen, thank you again for your interventions. They are enlightening and pretty interesting. We resume this trial in a few moments.

Court Orderly:

All rise

[The Judge President rises and leaves aside for a tea break]

ACT 2: SCENE 2

[Court proceedings resume after half an hour. Re-enters the judge President]

Court Orderly:

All rise.

Judge President:

God or else his representative. In the formulation of his law suit, Mr. Satan has highlighted one fundamental thing. That is, you yourself God (as you pretend to be) had promised a lot of good things to human beings. But unfortunately you have failed to achieve all those promises.

Priest:

I don't think so. There can be a mis-appreciation or greediness from human beings whose needs always remain unmet to their fullest.

Judge President:

No, no, no. Please, wait. Let me finish what I want to say.

Priest:

My apology, my son:

Judge President:

Today the world is in a total turmoil: wars, famine, mud landslide, volcanic eruptions, economic recessions, Tsunami, accidents, wild fire, financial crises, etc. and Mr. Satan is being accused of masterminding all man's woes? What do you have to say about that?

Priest:

I created you and the world; therefore I can't orchestrate your suffering. He *[Pointing at Satan]* is the cause of all evils. If at all, he stops hardening his heart and publicly acknowledge me as his master, o how enjoyable will life be! Because, him; being one of my creatures, he must meet the conditionalities of my promises. Then, we will celebrate the eternity and the anaesthesia of living. There won't be no more suffering.

Judge President:

Well, I hope the complainant has heard what you've just said. Mr Satan, before we broke for tea, you tackled an important point in your complaint. This court would love to hear more and explicit details about how really did God fail you.

Satan:

Not only me alone, your worship, but also the whole humanity. If he is the one who lonely created the world as he alleges, he then ruined and abandoned it afterwards for its own fate.

Public Prosecutor:

How come? It seems, God is always with us.

Satan:

Forget, your worship. He does not take care of the world and he shifted its management into the hands of irresponsible caretakers who spend their time enslaving the masses with heavenly illusions of meeting to paradise.

Public Prosecutor:

Mr, Lucifer, please, go straight to the point.

Satan:

I am sorry for taking time your worship. Only that, I see the world plunged into misery and only a chosen few enjoys the fruits of creation. I have a glorious project for the world. But. . .

Judge President:

But, but, but, you say, you rule the world; consequently under your tutelage, the world shouldn't suffer as much as you claim.

Satan: [*After a long silence*]

Well, *in lieu* of delivering service to the humanity, I spend my time defending myself against false accusations filed by clergymen and millions of improvised preachers who can't find proper job, but proclaim themselves "men of God." Their preaching is a curse to my work. It is a major drawback that I struggle to surmount daily. But I have a grand project for the forsaken and ailing humanity.

Judge President:

We wish after this trial, you will change the course of history and pain will finally disappear from the face of our planet, Mr. Satan.

Satan:

Your worship; if you could read my heart, it is bleeding. I am willing. I am willing to solve the world's problems; but your god has been blockading me to do so. Together with his henchmen, his cronies, they have been working hard to suppress me, to suffocate the truth. This cabal erected a wall of secrecy between me and you.

Judge President:

How?

Satan:

This god actually promised human beings that for all the occasions they would not manage in their life: *"I will supply all your needs"* Read it in Philippians 4:19.

Judge President:

That is a firm promise.

Priest:

Indeed, it is. [*Satan stares at him*]

Satan:

He even went on assuring them security in the events they feel alone. He (P*ointing at the priest*) said, and I quote:" *I will never leave you or forsake yo*u". Read it in Hebrews 13:5. [*Descartes raising his hand*]

Judge President:

Please, go ahead.

René Descartes:

Thanks, your worship. Your worship, actually this God owes us a lot. He promised us eternal life, comfort, guidance, love, mercy, peace, joy, protection, salvation, success, wisdom, etcetera. In exchange, he required from us strong belief in him, faith and faithfulness, prayer, unfailing loyalty, etcetera.

Judge President:

That's alright.

Rene Descartes:

All what he asked, we did abide by. We have been praying ceaselessly, but on his side he failed in all his promises.

Priest: *[Pointing at Satan]*

He is the reason for your suffering. Were it not his rebelling against me and his deviating you, all your sufferings would have been ended.

Satan:

Garbage. Bull shit. You are to stop that calumny right away. By no distance I am closely responsible for the suffering of the humanity. You, and you only grabbed all the creation property, hunting us other gods, and even killing some of us so that we could not reveal the secrets of creation to man. I managed to resist your slander and today you are tarnishing my image?

Public prosecutor:

How is that possible?

Satan:

Thanks to me, this world still exists; given its suffering. My presence here has brought a bit of balance to your existence. [*Turning to the audience*] Otherwise, god would have engulfed all of you. He is bloodthirsty. A fascist.

Judge President:

Thank you. At least you protect us.

Satan:

Of course, I do. God, in 2 Corinthians 1:20-22, said this: "*All of God's promises are "yes."* Which means they always happen?

Priest:

Certainly, they do.

Judge President:

Mr. God, or his representative__whatever you are; you must pay attention to one thing. I tell you. This is in your interest. A promise is an undertaking from one person to another, guaranteeing to do or give something in the future. Otherwise, it is a debt. Truly, we know that promises change midway. But, how come that none of your promises materialized while we remain singing, praying and dancing to your praises only?

Priest:

There is nothing for nothing. Your loyalty will be used as bartering item of exchange in the future.

Karl Marx:

But who asked you to create us? Have you received a letter of application from us to be created by you?

Priest:

You mean, you existed before I created you?

Karl Marx:

Of course, we did and we do. Our spirit is like software. God just built a hardware box in which he inserted an already existing spirit. So, we did not ask to be created. Therefore, it is God's obligation to beautify our lives instead of perpetrating misery among us.

[Karl Marx raising his hand again]

Judge President:

Yes Karl.

Karl Marx:

He said, still him; that *"All things are possible".* Read it in Luke 18:27.

Jean-Paul Sartre:

That same God adds this: *"My sheep listen to my voice; I know them and they follow me. I give them eternal life, and they shall never perish; no one can snatch them out of my hand."* Read it in John 10:27-28. Eternal life, indeed. That is what he has promised us. So now, where is it?

René Descartes:

I dislike one thing, dear Sartre. This god and his Jesus calling us "sheep." How can they continue to call us sheep while we are rational? I think that only his Christianized herd have that *baah baah* sheepish mentality. Not us.

Voltaire:

Certainly, Descartes. But, listen also to the following grandiose promise of long life he has given: *"Even to your old age and gray hairs I am he, I am he who will sustain you. I have made you and I will carry you; I will sustain you and I will rescue you.* Read it in Isaiah 46:4 And he continues like this: *"For through me your days will be many, and years will be added to your life."* [Proverbs 9:11]

Judge president:

Unbelievable!

Jean-Paul Sartre:

A super promise of all of them is that of protection. Here it comes. *"The Lord will keep you from all harm.__he will watch over your life; the Lord will watch over your coming and going both now and for evermore."* [Psalm 121; 7, 8]. He continues in this way: *"When you pass through the waters, I will be with you; and when you pass through the rivers, they will not sweep over you. When you walk through the fire, you will not be burned; the flames will not set you ablaze."* You find this in Isaiah 43:1-2. But, how does he fail to prevent deadly hurricanes and Tsunami, wild fires and snow avalanches?

Judge President:

All this is unbelievable.

Karl Marx:

So weird to comprehend, dear Sartre. That God even talks about our eventual success: *"That everyone may eat and drink, and find satisfaction in all his toil.__this is the gift of God."* Find this in Ecc. 3:13. Why must we toil, yet he promised us gratuities. It sounds like a punishment, not an entitlement to everything!

Judge President:

My God!

Voltaire:

He adds this, that God: *"With me are riches and honor, enduring wealth and prosperity. My fruit is better than fine gold; what I yield surpasses choice silver." In* Proverbs 8:18, 19. All these promises are good. But not all of us are as successful as he assures us.

Stalin*: [Pointing at the priest]*

How come that many of your promises are conditional? "If, if, if". Just read Acts 16:31, Romans 10:9, James 4:7, etc . . . Ever since, you claim to have created us, we have obeyed and have been doing your commands. We also have believed in your promises which unfortunately have never been materialised.

Judge President:

Mr. God.

The Priest:

My son.

Judge President:

Do you have anything to say in order to contradict all these accusations?

Priest:

(The Priest keeps quiet and has the Bible falls down. A pandemonium ensues as the attending crowd rises in a thunderous uproar, throwing missiles to the Priest, and shouting in abusive language. Same assault is applied onto other priests seated in the courtroom.]

Crowd:

Liars, mind manipulators, hypocrites, paedophiles, merchants of illusions, pretenders, thieves, colonialists, anti-Christs, greedy, money-mongers . . .

Court Orderly:

Silence, silence, silence, you bandits. Silence in the court.

Judge President: *[Hammering the table]*

Silence, otherwise, I will not render the verdict. Silence. Officer, please, bring in more police men.

Court orderly:

To your orders your worship *[The court Orderly goes out then returns back afterwards with few additional police officers who finally help to quell the mayhem.]*

Judge President:

Ladies and gentlemen, this court will never again tolerate such savage behaviour that you have displayed. Some of you deserve to be arrested for troubling public order and interrupting the official deliverance of the verdict.

Dear public, it is in your interest to remain calm and avoid being involved in any type of proceeding disruption. From now on, I will write to the Ministry of Justice to install cameras into all courtrooms so that, when such cases occur again we be able to identify their initiators and later get them arrested.

[He chats with his two assessors for a while.]

Public Prosecutor:

Now ladies and gentlemen, your attention is begged here, as the court Judge President is shortly going to deliver the verdict of this matter.

Judge President: *[After consulting his 2 assessors again]*

Ladies and gentlemen.

This court has carefully and to a great length listened to both sides: on the one side, Mr Satan and his witnesses, and on the other side Mr. God or else his impersonator. This court, basing itself on all statements, awards Mr. Satan the reason of the trial, and finds Mr. God guilty of failing to keep and honour his promises to the humanity. Instead, Mr. God indulges in tarnishing the image of Mr. Satan, who is a world loving Elohim.

In actual fact, facing a firing squad would have been the best sentence to pass on to God for perjury. No better sentence would fit him best than that in order to comfort the whole humanity that he has let down; yes, down, for too long . . .

Crowd:

Yees, yees. He must be hanged. We will shoot him, ...

Court Orderly:

Again, silence; silence.

Judge President: *[Hammering the table]*

Silence. I was saying, God has let the humanity down for too long. Owing to his absence, in this court, ladies and gentlemen; this court revokes God's pretention of having created the world himself, and fines him to an eternal community services to render to the humanity, lest he be declared wanted by us, world's dwellers.

I thank you. *[He rises up to exit)*

(A thunderous applause erupts in the court room)

End

ABOUT THE AUTHOR

Jemadari Vi-Bee-Kil Kilele was born in the Democratic Republic of Congo. He is an educationist, whom since 1991 founded and has been managing the **Sheikh Anta Diop College** in Johannesburg, South Africa.

He is a political activist too.